Jingle Bells,
Homework Smells

Jingle Bells, Homework Smells

Diane de Groat

HarperCollins*Publishers*

Jingle Bells, Homework Smells
Copyright © 2000 by Diane deGroat

Reprinted by arrangement with HarperCollins Publishers.
Printed in the U.S.A.

www.harperchildrens.com

Library of Congress Cataloging-in-Publication Data
deGroat, Diane.
Jingle bells, homework smells / Diane deGroat.
p. cm.
Summary: Gilbert forgets to do his homework over the weekend because he is busy playing in the
snow and getting ready for Christmas, but then he comes up with a solution at the last minute.
ISBN 0-688-17543-0 (trade) — ISBN 0-688-17544-9 (library)
[1. Homework—Fiction.   2. Schools—Fiction.   3. Snow—Fiction.   4. Christmas—Fiction.]
I. Title.   PZ7.D3639 Ji 2000   [E]—dc21   99-50291

3 4 5 6 7 8 9 10
❖
First Edition

To Bill. Wherever you are.

Mrs. Byrd was writing something on the board, but Gilbert didn't notice. It was hard to think about schoolwork when it was almost Christmas. Instead, Gilbert thought about what Santa might bring him. He thought about having a whole week off from school to play. He didn't want to think about spelling or math or—

"Gilbert!" Mrs. Byrd called. "Please pay attention."

Gilbert turned and saw that everyone had moved to the story corner. Everyone except Gilbert. He stumbled out of his chair and quickly found a spot between Patty and Frank. He would have to try harder to pay attention!

When everyone was settled, Mrs. Byrd read a story about a snowman that came to life. Gilbert wished he could make his own snowman, but it hadn't snowed in a long time. He hoped it would snow by Christmas. He had asked Santa to bring him a brand-new Red Racer Speed Sled. His old sled had broken last year when Lewis crashed into it on Daredevil Hill.

When Mrs. Byrd finished the story, she said, "The snowman is the main character. For homework I'd like you all to make a picture of a character from your favorite book. We can talk about the books and the characters on Monday."

Lewis groaned about getting homework over the weekend. He didn't like to read and he didn't like to draw, especially on a weekend. Gilbert liked to read and draw, and all afternoon he tried to think of which book he liked best.

Mother was baking cookies when he got home, and Gilbert wanted to help decorate them. "Do you have any homework to do?" she asked.

"I can do it later," Gilbert said.

But later he watched a holiday special on TV. He wasn't worried, because he still had the whole weekend to do his homework.

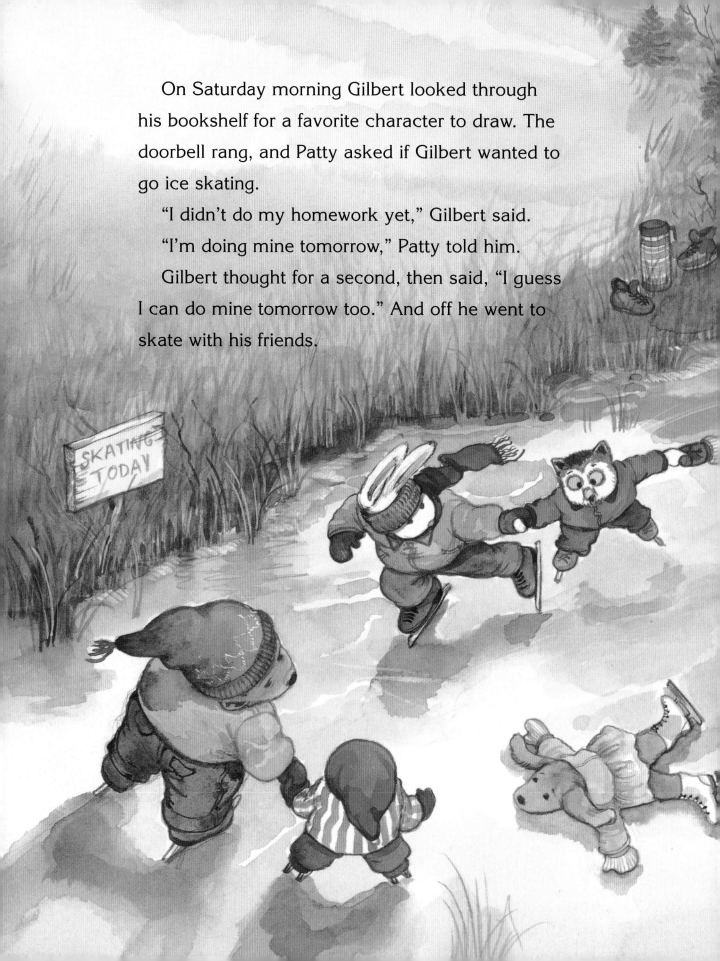

On Saturday morning Gilbert looked through
his bookshelf for a favorite character to draw. The
doorbell rang, and Patty asked if Gilbert wanted to
go ice skating.

"I didn't do my homework yet," Gilbert said.

"I'm doing mine tomorrow," Patty told him.

Gilbert thought for a second, then said, "I guess
I can do mine tomorrow too." And off he went to
skate with his friends.

On Sunday Gilbert and his sister went with Father to pick out a Christmas tree. Lola ran from tree to tree, saying, "This one. No, this one. No, this one's better!"

They finally agreed on one perfect tree and tied it to the top of the car.

After dinner they hung the decorations and drank
hot cocoa. Father read "The Night before Christmas,"
and Gilbert couldn't wait until Santa came. He couldn't
think about anything except flying down Daredevil Hill
with his new Red Racer Speed Sled!

It was snowing when Gilbert got up on Monday
morning. He hopped up and down with excitement.
After school he could make a snowman! Of course he
would do his homework first.

Homework!

Gilbert had forgotten to do his homework! He
hadn't chosen a book or drawn a character. Gilbert
had never forgotten to do his homework before. Mrs.
Byrd always gave him a happy-face sticker for doing
good work. He wasn't going to get a happy-face
sticker today! His stomach began to hurt.

"I don't feel good," he said to Mother when he went downstairs. "I can't go to school today."

Mother felt Gilbert's forehead. "Hmmm," she said. "You'll have to stay in bed then. And you won't be able to play in the snow."

Gilbert wanted very much to play in the snow. "I'll feel better later," he said. "I just can't go to school."

"And why is that?" Mother asked.

Gilbert said quietly, "I didn't do my homework."

"Oh, dear," said Mother. "You should have done it when you got home from school on Friday."

Gilbert whined. "But I had to decorate the cookies on Friday. And I had to go ice skating on Saturday. And yesterday we had to get the tree and Lola took forever picking one out. I didn't have time to do my homework!"

Mother said, "You still have to go to school, Gilbert. You'll have to tell Mrs. Byrd that you didn't do your homework." She made some warm oatmeal with extra honey, but Gilbert didn't eat it. He was upset because he couldn't stay home.

He finally put on his coat and boots and slowly walked to school. Patty met him on the playground. "What's wrong, Gilbert?" she asked when she saw his face.

Gilbert said, "You shouldn't have asked me to go skating on Saturday. I didn't have time to do my homework."

"I did mine," Patty said.

Suddenly a snowball flew right past Gilbert's ear.
"Snowball fight!" Lewis said as he caught up to them.

"Quit it," Gilbert snapped. "I'm not playing."

"Gilbert didn't do his homework," Patty explained.

"We had homework?" Lewis asked. Lewis always
forgot to do his homework. And now Gilbert was just
as bad as Lewis!

"We were supposed to draw a character like the
snowman in Mrs. Byrd's book," Patty said. "I made a
picture of Curious George. See?" She held up the
picture, then ran inside to show Mrs. Byrd.

"I'd rather make a real snowman," Lewis said. "It's more fun than drawing one." He scooped up a handful of snow and packed it into a big ball, singing, "Jingle bells, homework smells, teacher is a meanie...."

Gilbert didn't want to go inside either, and he began rolling his own snowball. That gave him an idea. But he would need Lewis's help to make it work!

Gilbert and Lewis ran into the classroom on the last bell. They had just sat down when Mrs. Byrd asked everyone to talk about the characters they had made. Gilbert sank into his seat, hoping that Mrs. Byrd wouldn't call on him. He wasn't sure if his idea would work after all.

Frank raised his hand and showed his drawing of the Cat in the Hat. Patty showed everyone her Curious George. Everyone had drawn a character except Gilbert and Lewis.

"Oh, my," Mrs. Byrd said. "I'm surprised at you, Gilbert." She didn't say, "I'm surprised at you, Lewis."

"Wait," Lewis said. "We did make a character. See?" He pointed to the window, and everyone turned to look. A snowman was looking back at them. A snowman with a red hat and mittens. "Gilbert and I made the character from the book you read to us. But we made a real one instead of a drawing!" He sounded proud that he had actually done his homework for once, even if it was Gilbert's idea.

Mrs. Byrd looked at Gilbert slouching in his seat.
She said, "Hmmm. Since it took two of you to do the
assignment, I will give you each half a happy face
for today."

Gilbert had never gotten half a happy face before
and he was disappointed.

Lewis had never gotten half a happy face before
and he was happy.

Then Mrs. Byrd added, "You can get the other half
if you do the assignment over for tomorrow."

When Gilbert got home, he didn't go skating or play
in the snow or watch TV. Instead, he drew his favorite
character.

And the next day there was a happy face on Gilbert's homework. And a smile on Gilbert too.